PENGUIN YOUNG READERS

Tiny Goes Camping

by Cari Meister
illustrated by Rich Davis

Penguin Young Readers
An Imprint of Penguin Group (USA) Inc.

This is my dog.

His name is Tiny.

Tiny loves to camp.

I do, too.

We need to pack.

We need a tent.

We need a flashlight.

We need food.

Oh, Tiny!
That is too
much food!

Where can we camp?

Not here.

Too many rocks.

Not here.

Too many sticks.

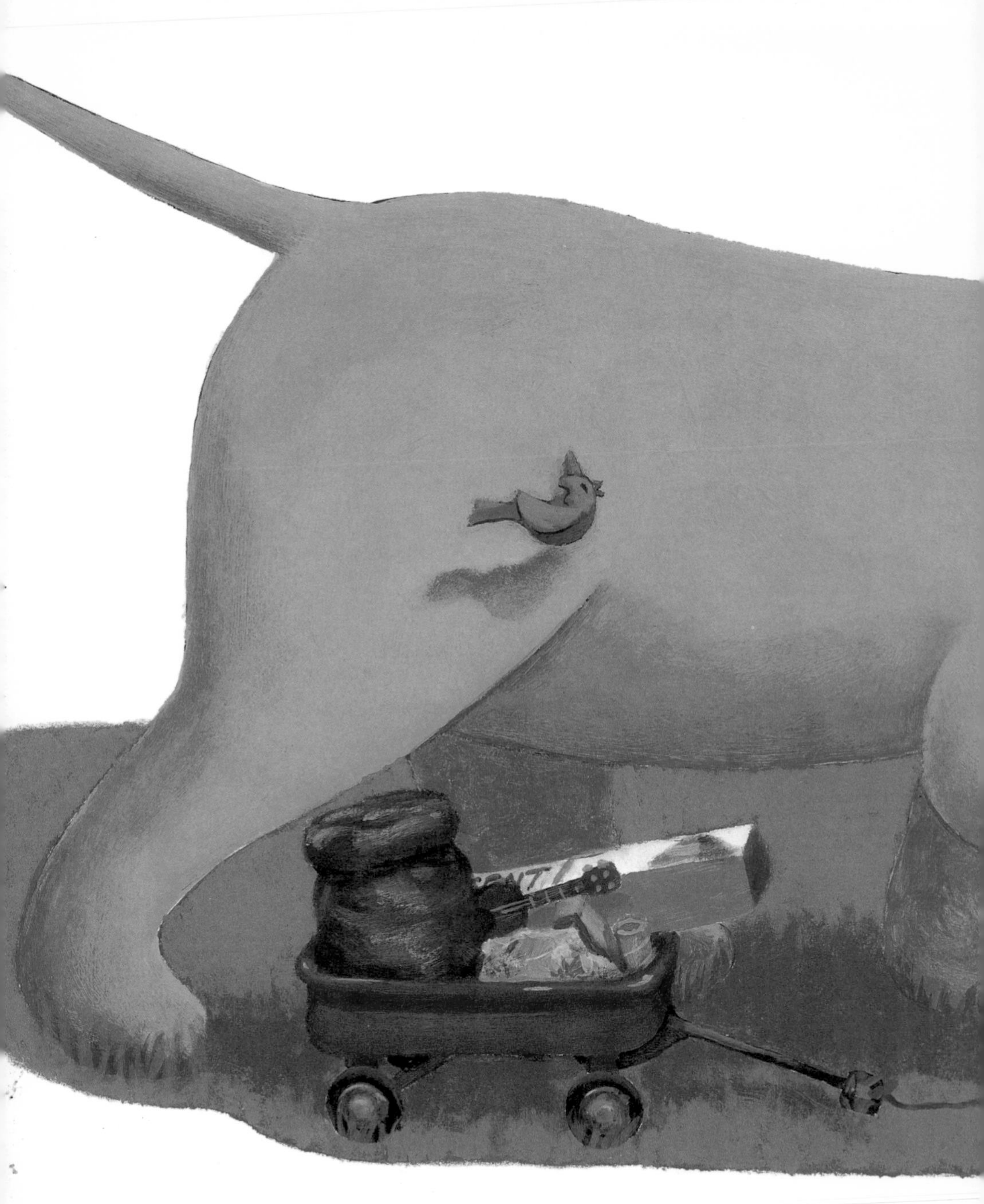

Tiny finds a good spot.

Good dog, Tiny!

We put up the tent.

We eat camp food.

We sing a camp song.

Tiny spots something.

What is it, Tiny?

A frog!

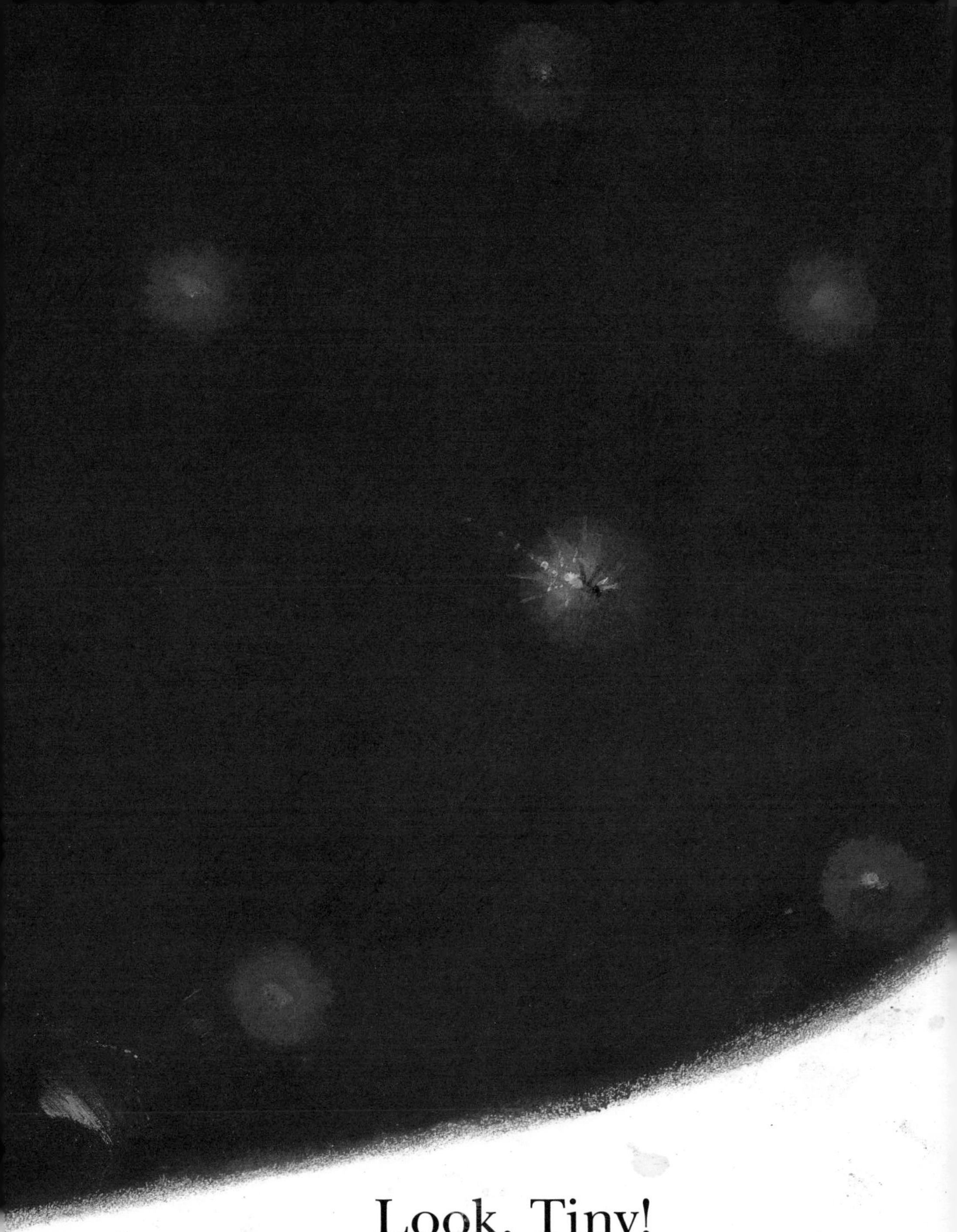

Look, Tiny!

Fireflies!

We chase them.

We catch them.

We put them in a jar.

Now we have a night-light.

Time for bed, Tiny.

Oh no!

The tent is too small.

POP!

Oh no!

That's okay.

Now we can see the stars.

Good night, Tiny.

Sweet dreams.